JUST MY FRIEND AND ME

BY
MERCER MAYER

W9-CPN-027

For Sam Gilpin

🏆 A GOLDEN BOOK • NEW YORK

Just My Friend and Me book, characters, text, and images © 1988 Mercer Mayer. LITTLE CRITTER, MERCER MAYER'S LITTLE CRITTER, and MERCER MAYER'S LITTLE CRITTER and Logo are registered trademarks of Orchard House Licensing Company. All rights reserved under International and Pan-American Copyright Conventions. Published in the United States by Golden Books, an imprint of Random House Children's Books, a division of Random House, Inc., New York, and simultaneously in Canada by Random House of Canada Limited, Toronto. Originally published in 1988 by Western Publishing Company, Inc. Golden Books, A Golden Book, and the G colophon are registered trademarks of Random House, Inc. Library of Congress Control Number: 87-81755
ISBN 0-307-11947-5   www.goldenbooks.com
Printed in the United States of America   First Random House Edition 2003
30 29 28 27 26 25 24 23 22 21

I asked Mom if I could have a friend over,
'cause I just don't want to play alone.

There are so many things we can do—
just my friend and me.

First we climb
the apple tree.

I could climb higher if I really wanted to.

Then we play in my tree house.
My friend says only babies use a ladder.

Next we play hide-and-seek.
I hide so well that my friend
won't ever find me.

We like to play with my racing cars.
They don't work very well in the water, though.

We like to play basketball, too.
I could get the ball
if I really tried.

Next we play with my new baseball
and my Louisville Slugger bat.

My friend likes to hit the ball,
but he doesn't like to chase it.

Then we have a jump rope contest.
My friend jumps a hundred times.
I could do that...

but sometimes I like to let my friend win.

We swing on my swing set, too.
Next time we'll swing on separate swings.

We take turns playing daredevil on my new bike.
My friend tries to stand on the seat.

It's only bent a little. I bet Dad can
fix it when he gets home.

My mom takes care of our cuts and bruises. My friend cries a lot. I only cry a little.

After we finish playing, we pick up my toys and put them away. My friend says he'll put away the comic books.

When my friend's mom comes to pick him up,
we say good-bye.

We always have fun when it's just my friend and me...

but sometimes it's great
just to be all alone.